AuthorHouse™
1663 Liberty Drive
Bloomington, IN 47403
www.authorhouse.com
Phone: 1-800-839-8640

© 2014 Maria Ana Lum. All rights reserved.

No part of this book may be reproduced, stored in a retrieval system, or transmitted by any means without the written permission of the author.

Published by AuthorHouse 10/15/2014

ISBN: 978-1-4969-4594-5 (sc)
ISBN: 978-1-4969-4595-2 (e)

Library of Congress Control Number: 2014918254

Any people depicted in stock imagery provided by Thinkstock are models, and such images are being used for illustrative purposes only. Certain stock imagery © Thinkstock.

This book is printed on acid-free paper.

Because of the dynamic nature of the Internet, any web addresses or links contained in this book may have changed since publication and may no longer be valid. The views expressed in this work are solely those of the author and do not necessarily reflect the views of the publisher, and the publisher hereby disclaims any responsibility for them.

I LOVE YOU LIKE A KANGAROO

By Maria Ana Lum

illustrated by Zeak McPeak

and
you can
be
adventurous.

I love you
like a
colorful parrot.

I love you like
a graceful giraffe.

You can feel
awkward sometimes,

and still
know you
are ok.

I love you
like a
cuddly
bear.

I will comfort you
so you can roar
and be strong.

I love you like a
soaring albatross.

You will break out
of your shell,

10

then you will be
on amazing
journeys.

11

I love you
like a majestic lion.
You can be adorable,

and
you are
brave.

I love you
like a bright-eyed owl.

You can ask many questions to become wise.

I love you
   like a
      playful monkey.
You can act silly,

and have fun
in everything you do.

I love you like
a shimmering hummingbird.

You are a precious jewel
and you see the
beauty in all things.

I love you like a smiling sloth.

You can be excited or

you can just chill.

21

I love you
like a leaping dolphin.

You can be joyful, and

you can be
a happy
friend.

to get up
and go, go, go.

I love you
most of all
because

you are being YOU!

CPSIA information can be obtained
at www.ICGtesting.com
Printed in the USA
LVIC06n0206281114
415922LV00002B/2

* 9 7 8 1 4 9 6 9 4 5 9 4 5 *